Under the Umbrella

Catherine Buquet • Marion Arbona

Translated by Erin Woods

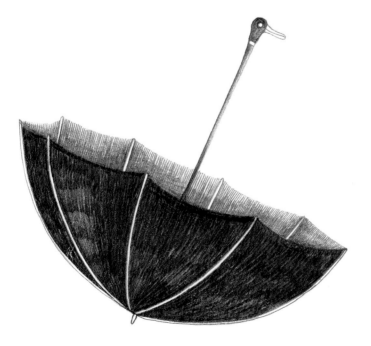

The publisher gratefully acknowledges the support of the Canada Council for the Arts and the Ontario Arts Council for its publishing program. We acknowledge the financial support of the Government of Canada through the Canada Book Fund (CBF) for our publishing activities.

Library and Archives Canada Cataloguing in Publication

Buquet, Catherine [Sous le parapluie. English]

    Under the umbrella / Catherine Buquet ; Marion Arbona

; translated by Erin Woods.

Translation of: Sous le parapluie. ISBN 978-1-77278-016-1 (hardback)

    I. Arbona, Marion, 1982-, illustrator II. Woods, Erin,

1989-, translator III. Title. IV. Title: Sous le parapluie. English

PZ7.1.B87Un 2017   j843'.92   C2016-904495-5

Publisher Cataloging-in-Publication Data (U.S.)

Names: Buquet, Catherine, author. | Arbona, Marion, illustrator. | Woods, Erin, translator.

Title: Under the Umbrella / Catherine Buquet, Marion Arbona ; translated by Erin Woods.

Description: Toronto, Ontario Canada : Pajama Press, 2016. | Originally published in French by Éditions Les 400 coups as Sous le parapluie. | Summary: "When the wind snatches a cranky man's umbrella and drops it at the feet of little boy outside a patisserie, the hasty curmudgeon slows down long enough for an unlikely friendship to blossom"— Provided by publisher.

Identifiers: ISBN 978-1-77278-016-1 (hardcover)

Subjects: LCSH: Friendship – Juvenile fiction. | Umbrellas —Juvenile fiction. | BISAC: JUVENILE FICTION /Social Themes / Friendship. | JUVENILE FICTION /Social Themes / Emotions & Feelings. | JUVENILE FICTION / Stories in Verse.

Classification: LCC PZ7.B878Und |DDC [E] – dc23

Manufactured by Friesens
Printed in Canada

Pajama Press Inc.
181 Carlaw Ave. Suite 207 Toronto, Ontario Canada, M4M 2S1

Distributed in Canada by UTP Distribution
5201 Dufferin Street Toronto, Ontario Canada, M3H 5T8

Distributed in the U.S. by Ingram Publisher Services
1 Ingram Blvd. La Vergne, TN 37086, USA

To Anne Da Cunha-Guillegault and Yves Nadon,
without whom this book would never have happened.
—C.B. and M.A.

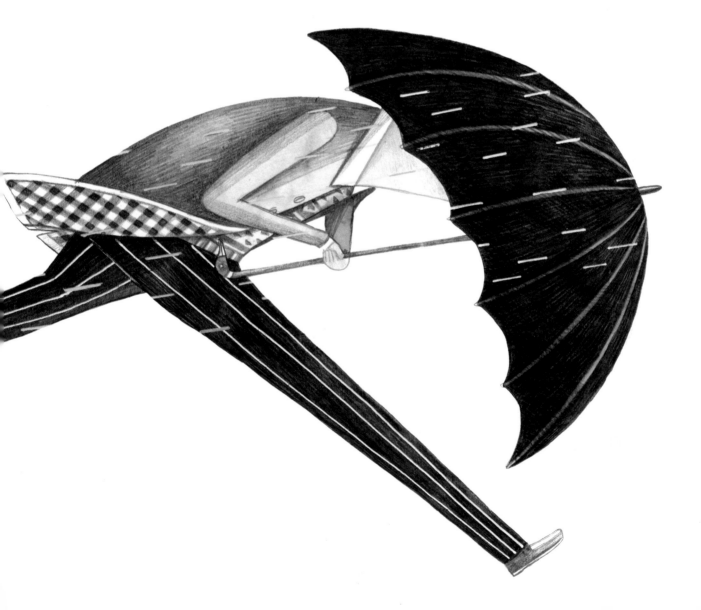

He grumbled at the raindrops
on the rooftops of the town.

He growled at the clouds
and at the crowds
that slowed him down.

Under his umbrella
He strode without a smile.
Under his umbrella
He muttered all the while.

His clutching fingers felt like ice.
His coat was splashed with mud.
Every step went *slosh* on cobbles
all awash, a-flood.

The wind attacked. He bent his back
and forced his way along.
Wet and cold and late—what else
could possibly go wrong?

With striding feet and stormy
heart he never even glanced
At a warm and glowing window
that held a boy entranced.

Dry beneath the awning,
he gazed upon the spread
Of cakes and creams and cookies
meant to turn each passing head.

The boy read every label, eagerly memorizing:
Macaroon, mousse, and Opera Torte—
who cared if the winds were rising?

But a sudden, stronger gust jostled the man across the street.
He stumbled. The umbrella

s w o o p e d . . .

s o a r e d . . .

s a i l e d . . .

And stopped at the little boy's feet.

Chasing the umbrella, the man ran fast and wild.
He muttered, dashed, splashed, spluttered—
then mumbled his thanks to the child.

The boy turned back to the window.
"Aren't they amazing?" he sighed.
The man couldn't help it. He
followed his gaze to the wonders
arrayed inside

A moment's hesitation—then he passed
the umbrella back.
He entered the store and returned
with a smile and a dainty paper sack.

Beaming at the boy's delight, he offered
him the treat:
A rich, red rhubarb-raspberry tart
that shimmered in the street.

Slowly, carefully, lovingly, the child unwrapped the ian.
Slowly, carefully, he broke it, giving the man the larger part.

Under the umbrella, time seemed to stall.

The rain fell on...
The sky hung low...
The crowds crept by...
And none of that mattered at all.